D0231901

MUDDY WATERS
PEARLY'S WELCOME TO LONDON

I'M ONLY SMALL, AND SOMETIMES TINY. I'M ON EVERY PAGE, CAN YOU FIND ME?

Pearly's Welcome to London

'Are we really going to London?' asked an excited and rather nervous Jolly Boatman.

'Yes. This is a very special journey, Jolly,' announced Muddy Waters grandly. 'It's about time you met your cousin, Pearly Whites.' Jolly had heard lots of tales about Pearly Whites and had always wanted to meet him. He was rather anxious about travelling on the River Thames after the frightening episode at the weir, but he was reassured to know that Muddy Waters would be with him all the way to London.

Jolly was so excited that he told everyone they passed that he was going to London. He bobbed and bumped around all of the different boats, explaining eagerly that he was off to meet his cousin. Some of the older boats knew Pearly well and enjoyed telling Muddy and Jolly about the wonderful times they'd had in the big city.

'London is a magnificent place, Jolly, but you'll need to be careful. It's very different from the Oxford Canal,' said Big Boris the pleasure boat.

The two boats enjoyed their time cruising down the Thames. Jolly was used to seeing beautiful buildings on his travels around Oxford, but as they journeyed further and further towards London, so his amazement grew.

Muddy liked pointing out such wonderful buildings as Windsor Castle, but he needed to hurry Jolly along. 'We'll have more time on the way back, Jolly,' said Muddy. 'For now, we mustn't be late for our meeting with Pearly.'

Before long, they arrived in the very heart of London. Even Muddy Waters, who had been to the capital many times before, always found the sights, sounds and smells very exciting indeed. Although Jolly was fascinated by all the new things around him, he stayed very close to Muddy Waters.

Suddenly, an unfamiliar blue and white boat pushed its way between them. 'Hello boys!' called out Pearly Whites, giving Jolly a little fright. 'Welcome to the most beautiful city in the world. It's really good to see you again, Muddy, and to meet my little cousin at last,' he said through a beaming smile.

'It's wonderful to see you too, Pearly, and to be back in London,' responded Muddy. 'I hope you're going to enjoy showing Jolly around on his first visit.'

'It will be my pleasure, Muddy. Sadly, I have lost something very special and would be grateful if you two could help me to look for it as we go.'

Pearly had been given a golden letter 'P' on a chain when he was a very young boat. He was proud of it and always wore it. He'd lost it a few days earlier and it made him feel very unhappy. 'I thought I had it somewhere near the wobbly bridge, by St Paul's, but I can't be sure,' he muttered.

The three boats cruised further up the river towards Tower Bridge where HMS Belfast was docked. Jolly had never seen such a huge ship before and he puttered nervously around him as they headed further into the river.

'Cedric is always going on about his time here in London and how he helped the big ships and boats when there was a war on,' said Jolly.
'Did someone mention Cedric?' asked Belfast in a very low voice.
'Er, yes it, it was me,' stuttered Jolly, amazed that such an enormous ship should know Cedric.
 'Tell him it's time he came to see me. I still miss the little fellow,' boomed the big boat.

Pearly was still anxious to find his chain. He searched frantically as they travelled further upriver dodging and darting around the bigger boats and barges with ease. Jolly however, was having trouble. Busy tugs had no time for visiting narrowboats, and roughly brushed them aside as they made their way to the docks. Even Muddy had to work hard to keep out of their way.

'Hurry up, Jolly!' Pearly shouted so all the other boats could hear. 'You need to buck your ideas up if you want to stay out of trouble.' This made Jolly very cross. He was trying hard to cope with the new challenges that surrounded him. Muddy Waters kept a careful eye on the two younger boats.

Jolly followed closely, keen to show Pearly that he could easily keep up with his cousin. 'Come on, come on, slowcoach,' Pearly barked, as he weaved his way across the river. Jolly sensed that Pearly was showing off and he soon grew tired of trying to stay with him. He felt as if he was working hard, without getting very far. He wanted to avoid bumping into any more boats and so he drifted further towards the riverbank.

Muddy Waters watched Pearly disappear further up the river, whilst he kept an anxious eye on Jolly Boatman. He called out to the little boat to come away from the bankside, but Jolly heard nothing above the noise of the busy river. Just as he would on the canal, he decided to pull to the side and take a rest. This was a terrible mistake.

Jolly had never encountered a tidal river before. He didn't realise that he needed to stay in deeper water, away from the mud flats at the side. Muddy Waters had tried to warn him, but it was too late. The little Oxfordshire boat soon found himself stranded and stuck firmly in the mud.

Pearly Whites turned around to see what had happened to his visitors. When he saw Jolly Boatman adrift on the mud flats, he laughed out loud. 'That will teach you! You're just going to have to wait there for a few hours until the tide comes back in,' he said as he puttered off, leaving a sad and lonely Jolly on his own.

As the tide drifted further out, Jolly's sadness turned to joy as he noticed something glisten in the mud. 'Is that a 'P' for Pearly I can see?' he gasped...

Much later on, with the water rising again, Pearly returned to help his younger cousin get back into the river. 'I might not be very good at keeping off the mud in the river, but I am good at finding precious things,' Jolly shouted to Pearly Whites.

Pearly noticed that Jolly had a muddy chain tied to his anchor. He took a closer look… 'It's my chain! it's my chain!' he shouted. He was so happy that he tooted, whistled and spun around until he felt quite dizzy.

'Oh Jolly, I really am sorry I called you a slowcoach. I should have warned you about the mud flats and the tide. Can you forgive me?' asked Pearly.

'Of course,' said a smiling Jolly Boatman, 'especially if it means you'll take time to show me this wonderful river and city,' he added.

As a special treat, Pearly Whites took his visitors further upriver than he would normally go. 'This is one of my favourite places,' he said as he stared up at the Thames Barrier. Jolly Boatman was very impressed, but wondered what it was meant to do. 'If ever the big floods come, this is what will save us. This stops all the water from getting to us up in the city,' Pearly told the Thrupp boats.

'It works like a huge canal lock, Jolly, although it is far more powerful', added Muddy Waters.

'Wow, it's amazing!' exclaimed Jolly.

As they travelled back up the Thames into the City, Pearly Whites enjoyed telling Jolly about his life in London. Passing the London Eye, he told Jolly and Muddy how he had helped to build it by carrying most of the parts along the Thames. 'It wasn't just me,' he added. 'There were lots of us helping and we all played our part. It was very exciting.'

Jolly gave an appreciative whistle. 'Do you think I'll be able to do anything like that, Muddy?' asked an eager Jolly Boatman.

'There's plenty to do on the Oxford Canal,' replied Muddy Waters. 'Although, nothing quite as grand as this perhaps.'

'I've never left London. I've never really wanted to until I met you, Jolly,' Pearly Whites told his younger cousin as they passed Battersea Power Station.

'Oh you'll love Oxford. It is very different and I suppose much quieter than London, but there's always lots to do,' said Jolly. 'Will you come and see us?' he added hopefully.

'I will. First, I've got some catching up to do. It was impossible for me to work when I lost my chain. I was too distracted. Thanks to you, Jolly, now I am able to finish all my jobs.'

Muddy Waters and Jolly Boatman said a fond farewell to Pearly Whites and to London. They all agreed to meet again at Thrupp.

Just as Muddy Waters had promised, he and Jolly took their time cruising back along the Thames. Jolly was sure he could find even more precious things, as he scoured the riverbank near Henley-on-Thames. 'Do you think I could find Ol' One Eye's treasure?' Jolly asked Muddy. His voyage to London had awoken a new sense of adventure.

Muddy frowned, 'We should steer clear of nasty Ol' One Eye and any thoughts of treasure. It only leads to trouble.'

'I'm not scared of Ol' One Eye,' said Jolly as he confidently puttered off towards Thrupp. But Muddy knew that an encounter with Ol' One Eye was looming and that Jolly's bravery would soon be tested.

Glossary

Weir: a low dam built across a river to control the flow of water

Pleasure boat: a fun boat that people can go on

Barge: a long flat-bottomed boat for carrying cargo on canals and rivers

Narrowboat: a canal boat less than 2.1 metres wide that is steered with a tiller not a wheel

Tug: a small, powerful boat used for pulling larger ships, especially in a harbour

Dock: a dock is a place on the wharf where boats are repaired and where they load and unload cargo

Tidal: water that has waves and that rises and falls at different times of the day

Mud flats: the muddy riverbed which shows when the tide goes out

Lock: gates on the canal which can be opened or closed to change the water level. Then boats can be raised or lowered as they travel through hills and valleys

Other exciting Muddy Waters stories to enjoy

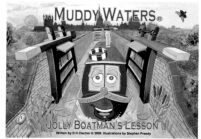

JOLLY BOATMAN'S LESSON

POPPY AT THE BOAT SHOW

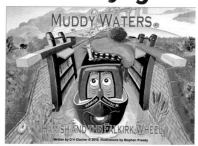

HAMISH AND THE FALKIRK WHEEL

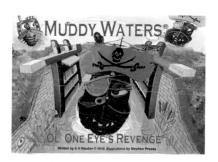

OL' ONE EYE'S REVENGE

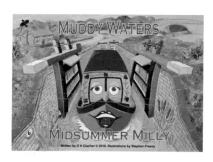

MIDSUMMER MILLY

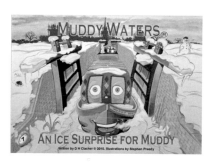

AN ICE SURPRISE FOR MUDDY

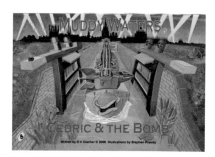

CEDRIC & THE BOMB

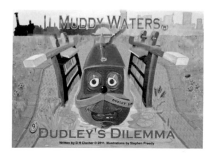

DUDLEY'S DILEMMA

OWEN'S DANCING DRAGON

www.muddywaters.org.uk..........

Stay **SAFE** near water -
Stay **A**way **F**rom the **E**dge

Go Wild Over Waterways - find games, learning and fun things to do at www.wow4water.net

The Inland
Waterways
Association

British Waterways

The
Waterways
Trust

people in print

Printed by Hunts (Oxfordshire) United Kingdom

MIX
Paper from
responsible sources
FSC® C004754

Printed on FSC (Forest Stewardship Council)
paper which confirms that the product comes
from legal and well managed forests according
to strict environmental standards.